F
MCG

McGuire, Leslie.

The terrible truth
about third grade.

1196
The Terrible Truth About
Third Grade
Leslie McQuire
AR B.L.: 3.8
Points: 1.0

F MCG

I hoped Ms. Sims wouldn't notice my math homework wasn't there.

But of course teachers always notice that sort of thing.

"Babette," she said, looking over the top of her glasses right at me. "Where is your arithmetic homework?"

"I don't have it," I said.

"Why not?" asked Ms. Sims.

"Well, I did it," I said. "But I asked my mom to check it for me. She stuck it in the script she's reading. She's going to be in a new play, you know. Anyway, she took it with her this morning by accident. It was stuck between the pages. I'll bring it tomorrow."

Ms. Sims got this squishy look on her face. Her mouth got all pinched together—sort of like a raisin. She was about to say something when Susie yelled, "Your mother isn't an actress! That's just another one of your dumb stories."

The Terrible Truth About Third Grade

Leslie McGuire

Cover by Susan Tang
Illustrated by Dave Henderson

Troll Associates

Z17530 7/93

Library of Congress Cataloging-in-Publication Data

McGuire, Leslie.
    The terrible truth about third grade / by Leslie McGuire;
illustrated by David F. Henderson.
        p.   cm.—(Making the grade)
    Summary: Bored with school, Jane, a precocious reader, neglects
her homework and alienates her classmates by making up incredible
stories about herself until her teacher, Ms. Sims, finds a creative
solution.
    ISBN 0-8167-2382-6 (lib. bdg.)   ISBN 0-8167-2383-4 (pbk.)
    [1. Honesty—Fiction.   2. Gifted children—Fiction.   3. Books and
reading—Fiction.   4. Schools—Fiction.]   I. Henderson, David F.,
ill.   II. Title.   III. Series: Making the grade (Mahwah, N.J.)
PZ7.M4786Te   1992
[Fic]—dc20   90-26788

A TROLL BOOK, published by Troll Associates

Printed in the United States of America.

10 9 8 7 6 5 4 3 2 1

*To Kathy J. with appreciation
for all your beautiful gifts.*

The Terrible Truth About Third Grade

Chapter 1

"*I* love October," I said as I walked out onto the playground with my friends. "It makes me think of France."

I was going out for lunchtime recess with Ellen Winston, Marybeth Hughes, and John Boles. They stared at me as I spoke. I could see that they did not believe me about France. I decided I had better say a few more things—just to make the story better. But first, I suppose I should tell you who I am. My name is Babette Simpson. I am the most interesting person in Southside Elementary School.

"My parents took me to France last year," I said. "They took me so I wouldn't feel so sad."

"What did you feel sad about?" asked Marybeth.

"Well, I don't like to talk about it much," I said. Then I looked down at my feet. "You see, that was the year my pony died."

"Oh, no, Babette," said Marybeth. "That's so-o-o horribly sad!"

"Gee, Babette," said Ellen. "What happened to your pony?"

Just then Susie Alton walked past us. Her nose was in the air. Susie's nose is always in the air. That's because she is so stuck up. She was with Warren Peach. Susie and Warren are both in my class. Susie thinks she is the prettiest girl in the world because she has long, blonde hair. I don't agree. Warren thinks he is the smartest boy in the world, but I don't agree with that either.

"Her name isn't Babette," Susie said with a nasty giggle. "Her real name is Jane."

I stuck my tongue out at Susie. Susie stuck her tongue out, too.

Susie knows my real name because she was in my second-grade class last year. Now, she's telling everyone in my third-grade class that my name isn't really Babette. I mean, what difference does it make to her? None.

I know the real reason she tells my real name. It's because Susie is a total rat.

My parents named me Jane. What a boring name. I have been looking for a better name for a long time. This year I finally decided that Babette is perfect.

Even Ms. Sims, our third-grade teacher, calls me Babette. Ms. Sims is nice. She is very tall, and sort of thin. She has reddish hair and she wears glasses.

It only took me a day to get Ms. Sims to call me Babette. All I had to do was not answer when Ms. Sims called me Jane. Then I would remind her that my name is Babette.

Of course, the first few times Ms. Sims forgot. She called me Jane again. But by the end of the day, she only forgot my name a few times. By the end of September, Ms. Sims seemed to have forgotten that my name was anything else but Babette. I wonder if she crossed out "Jane" and wrote "Babette" on her seating plan.

By the end of September everyone else in the class was calling me Babette, too. Everyone except Susie Alton and Warren Peach. But I don't really mind. I just don't answer them.

"See you later, *Jane*," Warren called.

I glared after Susie and Warren. Then I went on with my story.

"My pony's name was Blaze, and he was the most beautiful pony in the whole world," I said. "He once saved my life in a flood. But he got this terrible sickness from eating rose bushes. Then he died. I cried for a month."

Marybeth looked very sad. I felt bad about saying the part about eating rose bushes. Marybeth has a big soft spot for animals. But it made the story better, so I put it in anyway.

"Where did you get a pony?" asked John. He looked suspicious.

"My dad gave him to me," I said, looking gloomy.

"You must be rich," said Ellen Winston.

"My dad is rich," I said. Then I looked even gloomier. "But my parents are divorced, you know."

Ellen looked embarrassed, but John looked sort of interested. His parents are getting a divorce, too. I know because my mom told me.

"My dad is a really famous football player," I said.

"Neato!" said John. "What position does he play?"

"He's a quarterback," I said.

"I thought you told me he was something else," said Marybeth. "Didn't you say he was a tight end?"

I couldn't remember ever having said that. But Marybeth looked puzzled. Maybe I *had* said it once. My problem is I really can't remember what any of those football players are called.

"You must have gotten mixed up," I said quickly. "Quarterbacks are the smart ones."

John frowned. I guess he thinks all football players are smart.

Anyway, I guess I should tell you that most of the kids at school—except for my friends—think I lie a lot. But I don't lie. I just make up stories. You would make up stories, too, if you got as bored as I do. I mean, Southside Elementary School is not a very exciting place.

The kids are boring. No one ever has an exciting story to tell.

The school building is boring, too. It's got four "wings." Don't ask me why they call them wings. They sure don't look like wings. If they did, the building would be a lot more interesting.

First and second grades are in one wing. Third and fourth grades take up another wing. Fifth and sixth grades are in the third wing. Kindergarten and the art and music rooms fill the fourth wing.

There is a big, flat playground in back. All the grown-ups say a flat playground is good because it has lots of running space. But what good is running space if there is nothing interesting to run to?

The town I live in is pretty boring, too. It's called Greatdale, but I don't think it's so great. They should have called it Dulldale.

My mom and I live in an apartment. The only place in our apartment that isn't dull is my bedroom. I put lots of posters all over my walls. They are pictures of things I like to look at. I have posters of frozen lakes, Paris, the Amazon rain forest, and cute puppies. I even have one of kittens dressed up to look like a rock band.

My mom and dad are divorced. My mom works at a bank. She is a very nice mom. But I wish her job sounded more interesting. Banks are boring.

Anyway, I like to make up stories so things seem more exciting around here.

After listening to me for a while, Ellen and Marybeth and John decided to play on the swings. I would have gone, too, but there weren't enough swings for all of us. I decided to go sit under a tree.

Then I saw Marty Degan at one side of the playground. Marty collects rocks. He's always walking around looking at the ground. I decided that he might like to hear some good stories while he looked for rocks. After all, it must get pretty boring for Marty. All he does is stare at the ground.

"Hi, Babette," Marty said—once he noticed me walking with him. Sometimes it takes Marty a while to notice stuff.

"Find any good rocks?" I asked.

"Only one," said Marty.

He reached into his pocket and pulled out a gray rock that had some sparkly stuff on it.

"What's so good about it?" I asked.

"It's pyrite," said Marty. "Fool's gold is what they call it sometimes."

"Wow!" I said. "That's gold?"

"No," said Marty. "It just sparkles like gold."

"Too bad," I said. "Is there a lot of that stuff in the playground?"

"Yep," said Marty. "But sometimes it's hard to find. Mostly it's under the ground."

"You mean you have to dig for it?" I asked.

"Yeah," said Marty.

"That might make a neat story," I said. "You could say you'd discovered gold in the

16

playground. All the kids would start digging for it."

Marty didn't say anything. Maybe he didn't want all the other kids digging for his favorite kind of rock.

The bell rang. It was time to go back inside.

Ms. Sims said we were going to do some arithmetic problems. She handed out the work sheets. That's when I realized I had forgotten to do my math homework. I tried to race through the problems. If I got done early, I would have time to do the homework from last night.

But before I knew it, Ms. Sims had started collecting the math homework. I had finished the work sheet. But I only had two of the homework problems done.

"Now, boys and girls," said Ms. Sims. "Before we go over the work sheet, I'd like you to pass your homework to the front."

All the kids—except me—took out their homework. Then they passed it forward.

Ms. Sims walked along the front row and collected the homework papers.

I hoped she wouldn't notice mine wasn't

in there. But of course teachers always notice that sort of thing.

"Babette," she said, looking over the top of her glasses right at me. "Where is your arithmetic homework?"

"I don't have it," I said.

"Why not?" asked Ms. Sims.

"Well, I did it," I said. "But I asked my mom to check it for me. She stuck it in the script she's reading. She is going to be in a new play, you know. Anyway, she took it with her this morning by accident. It was stuck between the pages. I'll bring it tomorrow."

Ms. Sims got this squishy look on her face. Her mouth got all pinched together— sort of like a raisin. She was about to say something when Susie yelled, "Your mother isn't an actress! That's just another one of your dumb stories."

Everyone started to laugh. But I didn't care.

"She is, too," I said loudly.

"She is not," said Susie. "She works at the bank. I see her there all the time!"

"Lots of actresses work at other jobs

between plays," I said. "They get jobs as waitresses, or taxi drivers, or anything."

"Now, class," said Ms. Sims. "Quiet, please!"

She gave me another one of those squishy looks. Sometimes I think Ms. Sims doesn't believe my stories. But she never says anything. Whatever the look meant, it didn't matter. She had a hard time getting the class to be quiet. By the time things settled down, she had forgotten about my math homework. So I guess I should have thanked Susie for picking on me. It gave Ms. Sims another problem to worry about.

Karen Wiggs, who sits next to me, started scribbling in her notebook. Then she passed the notebook to me. It said: "Liar, liar, chicken frier."

Have you ever heard anything so dumb?

I guess some kids don't like me because I make up so many stories. But I don't care. Who wants a bunch of dull friends like them?

Chapter 2

Well, things stayed pretty boring until just before Thanksgiving. Then we went on this really great class trip. Ms. Sims took the whole class to the Museum of Natural History. That's in New York City. I wish my mom and I lived there. It sure is an exciting city.

We took the school bus to the museum. That was the only boring part. It is bad enough to have to ride the school bus to go home. But the ride home only lasts half an hour. The ride to the city took one and a half hours. But it was worth it anyway.

I sat next to Marty Degan. Nobody else wanted to sit with me. I didn't really want to sit next to them either. Besides, Marty is pretty okay. At least he's okay when he isn't looking for rocks.

We got on the highway. Even Ms. Sims knew this part was going to be boring. She said that we should all start singing songs. We sang "Michael, Row the Boat Ashore" and then we sang "Ninety-Nine Bottles of Milk on the Wall." I always thought that song was supposed to be about beer. I guess Ms. Sims thought that third graders shouldn't be singing songs about beer, so she changed it.

But then the bus driver started to get cranky. I heard him tell Ms. Sims that the noise was driving him crazy. He couldn't keep the bus on the road when it was that noisy. So we had to stop singing. That was okay with me. The singing was starting to make me crazy, too. Besides, I don't like sitting in school buses that are driving off the road.

When the singing stopped, I had a chance

to talk to Marty. I told him about how I got all A's last year. That's not *exactly* true. But I *could* have gotten all A's. I'm very smart, but homework is totally boring. So I don't always do it very carefully.

"That's really nice," said Marty.

"I also have this great doll collection," I said. "There are hundreds and hundreds of dolls in it."

I really *do* have a doll collection. My Aunt Sally gave it to me. There aren't exactly hundreds of dolls in it. But there are at least twenty-five.

"Wow," said Marty. "You have more dolls than I have rocks."

I guess he kind of liked the idea that I collected stuff, too.

"There are dolls from every country in my collection," I said.

Well, *almost* every country.

"I didn't even know there *were* hundreds of different countries," said Marty.

"There are *thousands* of different countries," I answered. "My Aunt Sally traveled all over the world. She went to Peru on a donkey. She went to Alaska on a dog sled."

"That sounds uncomfortable," said Marty. "Did she bring back any rocks?"

"Not that I know of," I said. I was getting kind of bored with that story. All Marty could think about was rocks.

"Last year I went to summer camp in Europe," I said.

"Oh yeah?" said Marty. "Where?"

"Yugoslavia," I said.

"I hear there are great boulder fields in Yugoslavia," said Marty.

See what I mean? Marty is really nice. But all he can think about is rocks!

Just then, things started to get interesting. We went over a bridge. We were finally in the city. I looked out of the window. There were lots of tall buildings and strange people all over the place.

And it was really noisy! Cars were honking. Trucks were screeching. I got a little worried about the bus driver. But he seemed to be doing all right. Maybe it was just singing that drove him crazy. If car noises drove him crazy he wouldn't last long as a bus driver, would he?

Anyway, as I was looking at all the sights,

I suddenly saw a really neat theater. It had a marquee out in front with light bulbs all around the edges. A big sign said, "Starting Next Week! *Southern Express*! All-Star Cast!"

"Hey look, Ms. Sims!" I said. "That's my mom's new play!"

Nobody even turned around to look. Snooty Susie turned up her nose.

"Her mom works at a bank," she said.

"Only during the day," I explained.

Marty was still looking out the window. He was smiling.

"I wonder why everyone in class isn't more excited about my mom's play?" I asked Marty. "After all, it isn't every day that you know someone who's going to be acting in a real play."

"Maybe kids don't know a lot about plays and stuff," he said.

I sighed. "I guess you're right."

We finally got to the museum. It was great to get off the bus. I felt like my legs were going to turn into pretzels after sitting in that school bus for so long.

The museum was neat. There was so much interesting stuff in there, I could have stayed for a year! Unfortunately, we had only a few hours.

We saw the dinosaurs, and the Hall of the Fishes. They had this giant whale hanging from the ceiling. John Boles asked Ms. Sims how come the whale didn't smell. Can you believe it? He actually thought the whale was real!

All Warren Peach could say was, "When is lunch?"

We also went to the part of the museum that had all these neat gems and rocks. I thought Marty was going to move in. Ms. Sims had to practically drag him out of there. It was a good thing we went to the rock room right before lunch. If Marty hadn't been hungry, he probably never would have left.

After lunch we saw some great animals that had been stuffed. They were in glass displays that showed where they lived and what the trees and stuff looked like. It was like taking a trip to Africa. That made me think of a few good stories.

There was one room that had elephants up on a platform. The big one in front looked like he was about to run right out the front door!

"My father shot that elephant when he was on safari in Africa," I said.

Ms. Sims just looked at me. Then Susie got in on the act.

"There's just another one of Jane's dumb lies," said Susie. "The sign right here says this elephant was shot in 1910. Your father wasn't even born in 1910."

I had to think quickly.

"What I meant to say is that my grandfather shot that elephant," I said. I looked down my nose at Susie. She thought she was so smart. But I am smarter. "It was just a slip of the tongue."

Well, that kept *her* quiet for a while.

The bus ride back home was worse than the one going into the city. That's because I knew we were headed back to Greatdale.

But when I got home, Samantha Peters and Jimmy Taggart were sitting on our front lawn, waiting for me.

Samantha is in second grade, and Jimmy is in first. Samantha has bright, carrot-red hair and millions of freckles. Jimmy has lost

his front teeth, and the new ones aren't in yet. He also wears huge glasses. I like them a lot. They are kind of my best friends. They believe *all* my stories.

"How was the museum?" Samantha asked. Her eyes were all round and blue. "I wish my class would go."

"We have to wait until we're in the third grade," said Jimmy, looking sad. After all, he had to wait two years for third grade. I guess two years seemed like a very long time to him.

I started telling them all about the planetarium. While I was describing how you could sign up to be in a spaceship that goes to Jupiter, some kids rode by on bicycles.

"Weird Jane!" they yelled.

"My name is Babette!" I yelled back.

"You only hang out with little kids because they believe your lies!" they shouted.

Samantha looked like she might cry, and Jimmy stuck his tongue out.

Who cares, I thought. At least Samantha and Jimmy are pretty smart for little kids. I decided to make the museum trip really interesting for them.

"The stuffed elephants were great, and so were the dinosaurs," I said. "But it was a pretty scary trip."

"How come?" asked Jimmy.

"Well, just as we were leaving the museum," I said, lowering my voice, "this bunch of guys wearing weird masks to hide their faces came up to us. They made the bus driver take us to a deserted warehouse."

"Omigosh!" said Samantha. Her mouth was as round as a donut.

"How did you get away?" asked Jimmy. His glasses had fallen down low on his nose.

"They made us all get out of the bus," I said. "But I saw a subway entrance right by the door to the warehouse. I told Ms. Sims to get all the kids down into the subway."

"Didn't the bad guys follow you?" asked Jimmy. He pushed his glasses up his nose.

"They couldn't," I said. "I led all the kids into the tunnel. It was so dark down there, they couldn't find us."

"Weren't you scared?" asked Samantha.

Her voice was so squeaky, she sounded like a mouse.

"Of course not," I said. "I just led the class underground through the tunnel until we ended up in the basement of the police station."

"Wow!" said Jimmy. "And then the police arrested the kidnappers?"

"Of course," I said.

"How did you know how to get to the police station if you were underground?" asked Samantha. She had a funny look on her face—like maybe she didn't believe me.

"It was easy," I said. "You see, a long time ago I memorized a map of the New York City sewer and subway system. I knew exactly where I was going."

"Wow!" said Jimmy. "How did you do that?"

"It was in the encyclopedia. I've read the encyclopedia from A to Z," I said. "I happen to be an awesome reader."

"Wow!" said Jimmy.

"Wow!" said Samantha.

Just then, I saw my mom coming up the

walk to our apartment. She looked tired. She's really pretty, for a mom. She has curly brown hair and big, blue eyes. But she was wearing a very boring suit. They make her wear boring clothes at the bank.

"Hi, Samantha. Hi, Jimmy," she called out.

Then she came up and gave me a kiss. "How was your day at school, honey?" she asked.

"Neat," I said. "We had a great time at the museum."

"Well, come inside and tell me all about it," said my mom. She started up the steps.

"I'll be right in," I said.

"Are you going to tell her about the kidnappers?" whispered Jimmy.

"Naw," I said. "That kind of stuff upsets parents. I don't think she could take it."

"Why couldn't she take it?" asked Jimmy.

"She has a heart problem from having had a bad fever," I said. "She was really sick when she was a little girl."

"Wow!" said Samantha, looking at my mom as the door closed behind her. "That's terrible."

"I have to go inside now," I said. "I'm a little tired from running around all day. Besides, I should wash my hands. Sewers aren't the cleanest places in the world, you know."

Chapter 3

*I*t really is true that I'm an awesome reader. What isn't true is the part about reading the encyclopedia from A to Z. Not that I don't read the encyclopedia a lot. I do. I just never read it from start to finish.

I read a lot of grown-up books, though. I like books about romance in the deep South, or during the Civil War. You can learn a lot of history reading grown-up books.

Unfortunately, I also mess up on my schoolwork a lot because I read too much.

Sometimes I think grown-ups have it backward. I mean, the reason they send you to school is so you will learn how to read. But if you already know how to read, you end up reading so much you don't have time to do your homework. Then you get bad grades in school. Then everyone gets mad at you because you are doing the very thing they sent you to school to learn how to do. This doesn't make sense.

Anyway, it was right before Christmas vacation that the trouble started. Ms. Sims asked me to stay inside for a few minutes during recess. She was holding an envelope in her hand.

"Babette, I'm worried about your homework," she said after all the kids had left.

I looked at my feet. *Uh-oh*, I thought.

"You do very well on the work I give you during the day," said Ms. Sims. "But you haven't handed in any homework for three days now."

"I keep forgetting to bring it in," I said. "But I really do it!"

"Did you remember to bring it in today?"

36

she asked. She took off her glasses and put them on the desk.

"I'm afraid I didn't do my homework last night," I said. "We had to visit my grandmother in the hospital. She had a heart attack."

My grandmother didn't have a heart attack, but she hadn't been looking very good lately. She *could* have had a heart attack.

"You always have some excuse, Babette," said Ms. Sims. "I am tired of so many excuses and so little work."

"I promise I'll do the homework every night from now on," I said.

I meant it, too. I really don't like it when Ms. Sims gets upset with me.

Then Ms. Sims handed me the envelope. A great big "uh-oh" was forming in my stomach. I knew that envelope would make my life miserable.

I didn't want to take that envelope home, but what could I do? I couldn't hand it back to her. That sort of thing just doesn't work with teachers. I put it in my backpack. I knew I would figure out what to do with it later.

"You can go to recess now," said Ms. Sims.

I walked slowly through the door and almost ran into Ellen Winston. Ellen, Marybeth, and John had been listening the whole time!

Remember the museum trip kidnapping story I told Samantha and Jimmy? Well, Samantha told Ellen's little sister, Kathy. Kathy told everyone in her second grade class. Next thing you know, all the kids in *my* class were laughing at me on the playground. Even Ellen, Marybeth, and John joined in singing, "Liar, liar, chicken frier." They turned out to be just like all the other kids around here. Boring.

Now they were giggling at me because I had gotten into trouble. I ignored them and went outside.

Usually the school day goes by very, very slowly. Today it zipped by as if it were wearing roller skates and going downhill. Before I knew it, it was time to get on the bus and go home. "You're gonna be in tr-r-o-u-b-b-b-l-e!" sang Susie Alton all the way home—right in my ear, too. Ellen or Marybeth or John must have told her about the envelope.

At least she was saying something else besides, "Her name isn't Babette. It's Jane."

My backpack was very heavy as I got off the bus. It was heavy because of that dumb note. But it was also heavy because it was the day I go to the library.

Luckily for me, the library is only three blocks from my house. That way I can go by myself. My mother is very busy. If I had to wait for my mother to take me, I would wait a long time.

I can go to the library whenever I want. But usually I only go once a week.

I like the library a lot. The ceiling is very high. There are big, tall windows with lots of little panes in them. It is always quiet at the library. It also smells good. It smells like books, and glue, and the shavings from inside the pencil sharpener.

Every week when I go to the library I check out two grown-up books. The next week I bring them back and check out two more. Miss Fredericks, the librarian, doesn't seem to care that I only take out grown-up books. I think she doesn't believe that I really read them.

Miss Fredericks is very pretty. She has curly hair, and she wears lots of eye shadow and big, dangly earrings. She looks very fancy for a librarian.

I started coming to the library when I was in kindergarten. By the time I finished first grade, I had read all the picture books they had. Last year, I finished all the books for kids in the third and fourth grade. I even read all of the books for older kids. Well, maybe not *all* of them, but at least all of the interesting ones. I had to move up to the adult section.

Whenever I bring my books back, Miss Fredericks always says the same thing.

"Did you enjoy them?" she asked as I walked in the door and put the books on the return desk.

She always smiles at me the same way, too. It's as if she thinks I'm very cute, but a big show-off. I *am* very cute. But I don't show off at all. Can I help it if I happen to be a good reader?

"They were really good," I said. "I liked the one about the Revolutionary War the best. It was about this lady who really liked Patrick Henry. Patrick Henry was an important man during the American Revolution. He said, 'Give me liberty or give me death.' But the lady who liked him got into lots of trouble. It turned out okay in the end."

Miss Fredericks laughed—very quietly of course. You have to be very quiet in the library. Then she patted my head as if I were a baby, or maybe a small dog.

"Are you planning to take out more books today?" she asked.

"You bet," I said.

"Why not look for something in the children's section?" she said. "You might find some books that are much more interesting for you."

"I've already read them all," I said. "But thanks for the suggestion."

Miss Fredericks smiled and shook her

head. She just started working at the library last summer. If she had been here for a while, she'd know that I've already read everything in the children's section.

I went over to a reading table and opened my backpack. I took out the dumb envelope from Ms. Sims. I thought it might be a good idea to read what she'd written to my mother before my mother read it.

But the envelope was sealed!

I sat down in one of the chairs to think. Christmas vacation was a few days away. If my mother didn't have a chance to talk to Ms. Sims for a couple of days, it would be too late. Then school would be closed for two and a half weeks. By that time, Ms. Sims would forget all about it. Right?

I decided to rip the letter up and throw it away. I made up my mind that I would do so much homework that Ms. Sims would be totally buried in pieces of paper that had my handwriting on them. She would forget there ever was a time when I *didn't* do homework. She would pray that I would *stop* doing homework, there would be so much of it!

I was going to get up and leave without checking out another book. But then I decided to see if there was anything new on the grown-up shelves. I had read most of the books up to "L." They arranged the fiction section by the author's last name. Of course, I didn't read every single book from A to L. Some of them looked pretty boring—even for grown-up books.

My eye caught a neat-looking cover. It showed a lady wearing a red ball gown. She looked very scared. The title was *Wild Flowers*. It sounded pretty exciting. I decided to take it out. I figured maybe if I took out just one book instead of two, I could stay out of trouble.

While the librarian was checking out my book I remembered I hadn't told her any good stories lately.

"My mom is opening in a new play next week," I said.

"Oh really?" said Miss Fredericks. She didn't even look up. "Which play is that?"

"It's called *Southern Express*. It has an all-star cast," I said. "Of course."

"Of course," said Miss Fredericks.

She handed me my book, and smiled sweetly.

"Are you going to be in the play, too?"

"They don't let little kids in plays like that," I said. "This play is in the big city, you know. It's not like in a church basement or something."

"I see," said Miss Fredericks. "Well, enjoy your book, dear."

I figured Miss Fredericks didn't know much about plays, either. Marty Degan was wrong about kids in Greatdale not knowing much about plays. *Nobody* in Greatdale knows much about plays.

As soon as I got outside the library, I ripped up the note from Ms. Sims. I looked around to make sure nobody from my class was hiding behind a tree or anything. The coast was clear. I dropped the pieces in the trash.

Chapter 4

*C*hristmas vacation came and went. My plan worked for a while. I did my homework every night, and I only read one book a week. Ms. Sims must have forgotten about talking to my mother. She didn't send any more notes home.

January came and went, too. I was really doing a good job on my homework. I decided that Ms. Sims must have thought my mom had read the note and gotten mad at me. Maybe she thought my mom was standing over me every night with a base-ball bat, making sure I did my homework.

Actually, my mom would never stand over me with a baseball bat. My mom and I get along really well. When she sees my report cards, she never makes a fuss about the bad grades. Once she told me that she realizes how hard it is to be a child growing up in a single-parent household.

My mom reads all these books about feeling better about yourself and how not to make your children upset about themselves, either. I guess her theory is that you should just say nice things to your kids all the time. That way, they get to like hearing nice things. Then they try really hard to be nice all the time. I think it's a good theory.

I was pretty good about doing the homework all through January and February. If I had a box of gold stars, I'd give myself fifty gold stars for good behavior for two months.

But by the beginning of March my life got so boring I couldn't stand it another second. Finally, I broke down and went to the library. I took out four books! Ms. Sims was lucky I even showed up for school that week.

After a week of not seeing any home-work, Ms. Sims gave me another note to take home. But giving me the note didn't work. I just threw it away again.

Throwing the notes away turned out not to be good enough. One day in the middle of March, Ms. Sims asked me why my mother was not calling her to set up a conference.

"Babette," she said, "I haven't heard from your mother. Is there something wrong?"

"No, nothing is wrong," I said slowly. "My aunt and uncle from Switzerland came to visit us right after New Year's. They were supposed to leave last week."

"Have they gone home yet?" said Ms. Sims. She looked a little annoyed.

"Not yet," I said. "They just love Great-dale. My mother is starting to worry that they might move in with us."

Ms. Sims's face got that squishy look that means she doesn't believe me.

"I can't understand it at all," I went on.

"I hear Switzerland is one of the best countries in the world. Why would anyone want to live in Greatdale when he could live in Geneva?"

"Well, America is a wonderful and exciting place," said Ms. Sims. She had gotten sidetracked. I can usually get her mind onto another subject very quickly. This time was no different.

"More exciting than Switzerland?" I asked. I looked amazed, as if such a thing just couldn't happen.

Ms. Sims got going. "Of course it is. America has wonderful theater, beautiful countryside, and very interesting and lively people. Your relatives probably just love the energy in this country."

"You're probably right," I said.

Then the lunch bell rang. I left as quickly as I could.

I thought the story about the relatives from Switzerland would help, but it didn't for long. Even though I handed in my homework, two days later Ms. Sims started again.

"Have your relatives from Switzerland

gone home yet?" Ms. Sims asked when I came in from recess.

"Yes, they left yesterday," I said.

"Good," said Ms. Sims. "Then I should be hearing from your mother shortly. Parent/Teacher Night is next Monday."

But Parent/Teacher Night came and went. My mom didn't show up. I guess I forgot to give her the flyer about it.

"I expected to see your mother last night," said Ms. Sims after Parent/Teacher Night was over. "What happened?"

"My mother sprained her ankle and the doctors think maybe she tore a ligament," I said. "All she can do is hobble to the car and back. She's in a lot of pain."

"Oh dear," said Ms. Sims. She looked upset. "How did that happen?"

"She slipped on the ice," I said. "It's the fault of the people who own our apartment building. They should have cleared the ice from the steps. Her boss at the theater says she should sue."

"Oh dear," said Ms. Sims. "I certainly hope she feels better soon."

"Me, too," I said.

Then the next day, Ms. Sims said she'd called my mom at home, but no one answered the phone.

"Are you sure your mother's ankle is sprained, young lady?" she said. "Or is this just one of your stories?"

"It's a miracle," I said. "Her ankle is cured. The doctors can't believe it. It's as if she never fell down at all."

"What a relief," said Ms. Sims. But she was squinting at me. I decided she wasn't buying the story. I had to think of something fast.

"Yes, it *is* a relief," I said. "Because Mom just went into rehearsal for her new play. They're opening in a month, and she has to be in the city every night and every weekend for two months."

By this time, it was almost April. I figured a month of rehearsals would move this conference up until May. Then being in the play would probably mean my mom would be busy for a year at least! Maybe for the rest of the time I was in school!

Ms. Sims called me outside the classroom. I guess she wanted to have another talk.

But as soon as I stepped outside, bells started clanging like crazy. There was a fire drill—thank goodness. By the time we all got back, we had to go to assembly, and then it was time to go home. I was saved, but not for long.

The next day, Ms. Sims didn't let me go to lunch with everyone else.

"Now, Babette," she said. "I realize things are hard for you."

"They are," I said.

"But it's very important for me to talk with your mother. I'm worried about you. I would feel awful if I let your schoolwork slide to the point of no return."

What was that supposed to mean? How can you get to a point of no return in schoolwork? Schoolwork just keeps returning—day after day, week after week.

"I feel I wouldn't be doing my job if I let this go on," said Ms. Sims. "I was sure your mother would come in on Parent/Teacher Night. I added a special note for her on the flyer."

"She really tried to make it," I said, "but . . ."

Ms. Sims didn't let me finish.

"I'm going to have to call your mother at work and speak to her personally," she said.

I gulped. This was going to be difficult. But then I had an idea!

"I wouldn't do that if I were you," I said. "They're having a big problem down at the bank."

"Oh really?" said Ms. Sims. "Now what would that be?"

"Well, you see, the bank president is suspected of having embezzled—that means stolen—all the bank's money. He and everyone who works at the bank are under house arrest. They can't leave until the police and the FBI and the IRS finish questioning them. My mom is really mad. She has to go to rehearsals and they may have to change the opening date of the play because she's the star—"

"Babette!" yelled Ms. Sims. "I have had about enough of your stories!"

I shut my mouth.

"Young lady, you are not going out for recess today—or for the rest of the term, either," she said sternly. "You will eat lunch in the classroom, and you will clean erasers every day until the end of the year. And I am going to call your mother tonight at home and tell her exactly what you've been up to!"

Then she handed me two chalk-filled erasers and said, "Get to work!"

I hate cleaning erasers. You want to talk about boring? Cleaning erasers is even worse than having kids yell, "Liar, liar, chicken frier." Yeccch!

Chapter 5

*W*ell, there I was, me and about five hundred grubby erasers. Well, maybe not five hundred, but it sure *felt* like five hundred.

"And I want to see every eraser clean as a whistle by the time I get back," Ms. Sims said, looking at me over the top of her glasses. "No excuses."

"What about my lunch?" I asked.

"You may eat your lunch at your desk," she said.

I was about to say I didn't bring my

lunch. I thought maybe I could tell Ms. Sims I had to buy lunch in the cafeteria. But then I realized I didn't have any money to buy a school lunch with. I was just going to have to eat the peanut butter and jelly sandwich my mother made for me.

Ms. Sims walked out the door. She said she was going to the teachers' lounge to calm her nerves.

I sat down at my desk and got out my lunch. I wished I had something to read. I always like to read a book when I eat by myself. It keeps me from getting bored. But the grown-up book I had from the library was at home. It's a mystery written by a lady named Agatha Christie.

It was the first grown-up mystery I had ever read. I really liked it. There were a lot more books by her in the library. I couldn't wait to read them all! Anyway, just as I was biting into my sandwich and wishing I had someone to talk to, Susie Alton came running through the door.

She was someone to talk to. Sort of. But someone else would have been a lot better.

"What's wrong?" asked Susie. "Did you do something *really* bad this time?"

"I never do anything bad," I said with my mouth full.

My mother always tells me I shouldn't talk with my mouth full because it's rude. I don't like being rude. But since Susie was rude first, I figured it was okay in this case.

"Then why are you eating lunch in the classroom?" she asked.

"My knee hurts too much to walk on it," I said.

"What happened?" she asked. She had her hands on her hips and her head tilted way over to the side. She looked like a parakeet. I bet her mother does that all the time, and that's why she does it. "Did you fall off Mount Everest on a hiking trip or something?"

"No," I said, swallowing another mouthful. "I hurt my knee in a car accident in France last summer. Every now and then it bothers me."

"I bet," said Susie with a sniff.

"So what are *you* doing in the classroom during lunch?" I asked. "I thought kids weren't allowed in here without a teacher's permission."

"Ms. Anderson gave me permission," Susie said in her snootiest voice. "I left my lunch money in my backpack."

"That sounds like a story to me," I said in *my* snootiest voice.

"Well, it isn't," said Susie.

She stomped over to her desk and reached into her backpack. Susie's desk is next to mine. As she unzipped the backpack, a little book fell out onto the floor. It opened to a page with a drawing on it. The drawing was of a baby chewing a rattle.

Susie didn't notice it falling. So I reached down and picked it up. There were lots of drawings of babies in it. There were a couple of drawings of a dog, too.

Suddenly Susie saw me looking at it. "Hey!" she said, snatching it from me. "Give that back. It's mine!"

"What is it?" I asked.

"It's my sketchbook," Susie said, turning red.

"Now *you're* making up a story," I said with a sniff. "You probably took it from somebody."

"I did not!" she said loudly. Then she stuffed it back into her backpack.

"You can't draw that well," I said. "I bet you couldn't draw a picture as good as this if you had art lessons for ninety years!"

The drawings were really, really good. They were almost like photographs. That's how I knew she was making up a story.

"Who cares what you think?" she said. "They are pictures of my little brother."

"I never heard you say anything about a little brother," I said, taking a bite of my sandwich. "You don't even *have* a little brother."

"I do, too," she yelled, turning redder. "My dad and his new wife just had a baby."

"Right," I said. "And this is their dog, I suppose."

"Yes, it is," she said, looking really mad.

"If you can draw pictures this good, how come you never draw in class?"

"There's nothing good to draw in class,"

Susie said. That was true, but it still sounded like a story to me.

"I say you took it from somebody else," I said. "But who cares?"

Susie just gave me a snooty, red-faced look. I bet she was red-faced because she was making up a dumber story than even I had ever made up.

"Who cares whether you believe me or not?" she said loudly. Then she left with her lunch money.

I was glad to be by myself. Being alone is better than being with Susie Alton any day. I figured I had better hurry up and eat or else I would never get to the erasers. But just as I finished my box of juice, Ms. Sims came back in the room.

Uh-oh, I thought. Now I'm really in for it.

"I haven't finished them yet!" I said. Ms. Sims hadn't even asked.

"I have homework papers to go over," said Ms. Sims. "Besides, I wanted to have a little talk with you."

Double uh-oh, I thought. I have noticed that whenever a grown-up wants to have a "little talk," it's never a good thing. I have also noticed that the best way to handle a "little talk" is not to talk at all. But that only works if the grown-up doesn't ask you any questions.

So, of course, that was the first thing Ms. Sims did.

"Can you just tell me the *real* reason why you don't do your homework, Babette?" said Ms. Sims.

She sat at her desk and got comfortable. She folded her hands in front of her and got that "I'll just wait until you're ready to tell me the truth" look on her face. I could see there was no point in telling her any stories. She probably wouldn't like them anyway.

"It's boring," I said.

"Boring?" said Ms. Sims. "Why do you think that? After all, teachers and parents work very hard to make things interesting for the students."

"I know," I said. "But everything is still boring."

"Sometimes in life, people have to do things that they don't like," said Ms. Sims.

"Just because something is dull doesn't mean that you can simply refuse to do it."

"I know," I said. I could feel a long lecture coming on.

"Are there any special problems at home?" Ms. Sims asked. "Is there something happening between your parents that you don't want to talk about? Is that the reason you don't do your homework?"

I tried to think if there was anything I could say, but there wasn't. Things at home were just fine.

"Everything is okay," I said. "I just get bored at school. The work isn't that interesting."

"Everyone gets bored with work," said Ms. Sims. "Even I get bored with work. Some days I would much rather play tennis, or sail a boat. But I come to school every day and do my job anyway."

That was pretty surprising. It never crossed my mind that teachers would rather do something else besides teach. I always figured they didn't have anything better to do. Maybe Ms. Sims was more exciting than I thought.

"But it's so hard to keep my mind on schoolwork," I said finally.

"What do you do that's more interesting at home?" asked Ms. Sims. "Do you watch television?"

"I read books," I said.

"If you like to read, why don't you read what I give you for homework?" asked Ms. Sims.

"Because what you give us to read for homework is *really* boring," I said.

This was not going well. Ms. Sims was looking grouchier by the minute.

"Perhaps you can help me make it more interesting," said Ms. Sims. "I thought *Pepito's Burro* was a very good story. What, in your opinion, is wrong with it?"

"It isn't that there's anything wrong with that story, Ms. Sims," I said. "It's just that it's so short. And it's also kind of simple, if you know what I mean."

"Not exactly," she said. "You mean the words are too simple for you?"

"That, too," I said. "But also, Pepito doesn't do much. Nothing happens to him. He just has a little burro. So what?"

"And what books do you read that are more interesting?" said Ms. Sims.

"I just finished a neat book called *A High Wind in Jamaica*," I said. "And now I'm in the middle of a really good mystery by Agatha Christie. It's about a murder on this train called the Orient Express. Nobody can get off the train, so the murderer is someplace in there with all the good guys. . . ."

Ms. Sims looked at me as if I had just turned into a giant lizard or something.

"What did you like about *A High Wind in Jamaica*?" asked Ms. Sims.

"I liked how all these little kids were able to drive a whole ship full of pirates totally crazy," I said. "I like it when kids turn out to be tougher than grown-ups."

Ms. Sims smiled. "I liked that book, too," she said. "Kids are stronger than most adults think they are, aren't they?"

After that, we talked about all the books I've been reading. It turned out that Ms.

Sims had read a lot of the same books. It was the weirdest conversation I'd ever had with a grown-up.

It was so strange that I totally forgot to tell Ms. Sims that Susie Alton had taken somebody's drawing notebook. Not that I'm a tattletale. I just thought it might be a good idea to get someone else in trouble for a change.

Then Ms. Sims said the weirdest thing of all.

"I have a great idea, Babette," she said. "Instead of giving you the same homework that I give the rest of the class, I'm going to give you something different."

Here's where I get into major big trouble, I thought. I scrunched my face up and waited for the bomb to drop.

"I want you to write a book of your own," said Ms. Sims. "Every night, instead of the usual reading homework, I want you to go home and write a grown-up story that's very, very long."

"You mean with chapters and every-thing?" I gulped.

"Exactly," said Ms. Sims. "After all, I can

tell from the crazy stories you've been telling me all year that you have a wonderful imagination."

She said this with a funny, crooked smile. Then the smile got bigger.

"But I think you should know that it's wrong to make up stories to get out of doing work," she said. "So there is one other little problem we need to take care of."

I wondered why she was smiling. I wasn't smiling at all. Here I had been thinking I was off the hook. But Ms. Sims wasn't letting me off at all. She was probably going to make me wiggle a lot more before she was done.

"I still want to talk to your mother—and soon, Babette," she said. "So I'm going to call her in for a parent/teacher conference anyway."

"But I really will do my homework," I said. I did *not* want my mom to talk to Ms. Sims.

"Don't worry, dear," she said. "Your mom won't be angry."

That's what she thought.

"What about the erasers?" I asked as the bell rang.

"Don't worry about them," said Ms. Sims. "You have a lot of work to do. You can't waste your time cleaning erasers when you have a novel to write!"

Chapter 6

I started writing my novel on April 10th. It was the night of my mom's parent/teacher conference with Ms. Sims.

It took more than a week for Ms. Sims and my mom to get together. That's because my mom *was* busy—she really *did* have a play to rehearse for. Of course, it wasn't a big hit show in the city. But it was still a real play.

You see, my mom always wanted to be an actress. So she tried out for a part in a play that the little theater group in town was putting on in the church basement.

Well, she got the part! Maybe she'll be a big movie star someday.

While my mom and Ms. Sims were trying to figure out when to meet, I was trying to figure out what to write a novel about.

That part was a lot harder than I'd thought it would be. I have read every book ever written. Well, not *every* book, but a lot of books. But reading someone else's book is pretty easy. Figuring out how to write one yourself is not so easy at all.

The stories I make up to keep from getting bored are pretty good. But they're awfully short. Novels are two hundred pages long! I don't know how writers make their books so long.

I thought about all the books I had ever read. I thought about what I liked best about each book.

I like history books, but to write one you have to know what was going on in the old days. You have to know what people wore, and what kind of houses and machines they had then. If I wanted to write a book like that, I would actually have to read some real history books! That's the same as doing homework! Ms. Sims is very sneaky, you know.

That left the love stories or the mysteries. I didn't feel like writing a love story. They have people going to all these fancy restaurants, and taking planes to Europe, and stuff like that.

The fanciest restaurant I was ever in was Nell's Steak House on Route 43. It was nice, but it sure wasn't very romantic. And I've never been in an airplane in my life. You have to have done something in order to write about it, I think.

That left writing a mystery. Now, I think mysteries are great, but murder mysteries are the best. The problem is, I don't know anything about guns, or knives, or poisons, or getaway cars, either.

So what *do* I know about? I only know about one thing, and that's Southside Elementary School. That's not much.

After thinking for a week, I still hadn't decided what to write about. I was feeling really gloomy about it one day on the playground. I sat on the swings and watched all the kids run around. Then I started to think about the kids and what they always did. You see, each kid has some kind of interesting, weird habit.

Marty Degan collects rocks. John Boles asks a zillion questions. Karen Wiggs sniffles all day long. Warren Peach always says he's hungry. The more I thought about them, the more interesting each kid got.

Suddenly, I thought about what would happen if we were all stuck together on an island someplace—sort of like the *Swiss Family Robinson*. I wondered if any of our habits would come in handy on the island. Maybe I wasn't looking at people right. Maybe rock collecting *could* actually be helpful sometimes.

That's when it came to me!

I would write a book about the whole class going on a long trip—maybe to Disney World. Then the tour boat gets hijacked by some bad guys. And we drive them all crazy with our weird singing, noise-making, back-talking, and whining about being hungry all the time. Finally, the hijackers put us off on some deserted island in the Florida Keys because they can't stand having us around for another second. And we all manage to survive and build shelters and stuff until we get rescued!

I went right back to the classroom. I made notes all during math. I made notes during assembly. I even made notes on the bus home. I forgot all about the parent/ teacher conference until I got home. Then I saw the note my mom had left on the refrigerator.

It said, "Seeing Ms. Sims tonight after work. Be home later. Eat the leftover meatloaf if you're hungry. Love, Mom."

Whoops! This was the big night. Suddenly, I felt awful. I wished I had done my homework like a regular kid. I wondered if my mom would be mad at me. Or worse, she might be worried about me. She had enough things to worry about without having to worry about me, too.

But just when I was beginning to get upset about upsetting my mom, I remembered something that I wanted to put in my book. It was neat how easy it was to forget about my own problems when I had something really fun to think about—like writing!

I decided I would make Warren Peach the pest who drives the hijackers totally off the deep end. All Warren ever does is ask about food. That could drive even the worst criminal crazy.

As I was making notes, I remembered that Ms. Sims should be in the book, too. After all, why would the whole class go on a trip without their teacher?

I decided she had to get sick, or something. If Ms. Sims couldn't take care of us, we would have to figure out a way to take care of ourselves and her, too.

I just couldn't wait another second. I got out the nice new notebook Ms. Sims had given me to start my novel in. On the first page I wrote, "THE WORST CLASS TRIP EVER, Chapter One."

Then I started writing. I couldn't write fast enough to keep up with the story inside my head. It was like a movie running right behind my eyes. I was afraid I would forget how I wanted it to go, so I grabbed a scrap of paper and made some more notes.

I called myself Amber in the story. I got to the part where I noticed these really weird looking men on the boat. They were wearing long raincoats, which was totally dumb in Florida in June. Their coats were all lumpy. I said to Marty Degan (who I called Tex in the story) that unless those guys had a really great rock collection under their coats, I would be willing to bet they were carrying submachine guns.

Just then the door slammed.

My mom was home.

I looked up and noticed that it was dark outside already. When I looked at the clock, I saw that it was almost seven-thirty! I had been writing for three and a half hours, nonstop. I had even forgotten to get hungry. I hadn't even worried about what Ms. Sims was saying to my mom. I had forgotten everything but the story!

But now I remembered everything. I was hungry and I didn't really want to talk to my mom about the parent/teacher conference.

Before I could escape into the bathroom or the closet, Mom came into my room.

"Oh, Janey, you sweet little thing!" she said, giving me a kiss on the head.

I guess I don't have to tell you that my mom doesn't call me Babette.

"Hi, Mom," I said, looking glum.

"Ms. Sims is very nice," said my mom. "And she thinks a lot of you, too."

I almost fell off my chair. "She does?" I said.

"Oh, yes," Mom said. "And I'm going to call you Babette from now on. I never knew you didn't like to be called Janey."

I felt pretty bad right then. After all, my mom had named me Jane. I didn't want to tell her I thought her idea of a good name was dumb.

"It will be like having a stage name," she said warmly. "Lots of actresses have them. Maybe you can help me think up a good stage name for myself, too."

"You mean, for when you get famous?" I said.

"Of course," said my mom. "Now come into the kitchen with me while I make some dinner."

Here comes the bad part, I thought as I

helped her chop carrots for a salad. This is when she tells me what a rotten kid I am.

But that isn't what happened at all.

"Ms. Sims says that you are a gifted child," Mom said as she stuck the meatloaf in the microwave. "Please get out the knives and forks."

My mom does that a lot. She tells you a story all broken up with chores, and complaints, and stories about something else.

"She says she feels that you may need special teaching, or perhaps you should skip ahead a grade."

"I don't want to get skipped ahead," I said. "I'm already the littlest kid in the third grade. In the fourth grade, I'd look like a midget."

"Don't worry," said Mom. "I told her the same thing. But she still thinks you might need something extra because you are bored with third-grade work."

Well, I knew that. I just didn't know that anyone else did.

"And she told me you are writing a book!" said Mom. "I would love to see what you've written so far! Actually, I'm a little hurt that you didn't tell me about it."

"I didn't start writing it until tonight," I said. "Besides, I thought you would be mad at me for not doing my homework."

"Ms. Sims says that many gifted children don't do homework, and they get bad grades for that reason," said my mom. "She says they are so far ahead of everyone in the class, they get bored. And then they get lost in their own thoughts."

Well, *that* certainly was true.

"Ms. Sims told me that Albert Einstein—who was the smartest scientist ever, and won the Nobel prize for physics—got a c in physics when he was in school!" said my mom with a laugh. "Does that make you feel better?"

It sure did.

After dinner, Mom read my story. I told her what was going to happen next. She liked it!

"I think you should show Ms. Sims what you've written," she said as she tucked me into bed. "I don't want her to think you aren't doing anything at all for homework, you know."

The next day, I handed the notebook to Ms. Sims right before lunch.

"So you finally did some homework?" Marty asked as we went outside for lunch.

"No, that was my novel," I answered.

John Boles was walking right behind us. He heard what I said. So he butted in, of course.

"Kids don't write novels," he said.

"Ms. Sims asked me to write a novel instead of doing the homework all the rest of you do," I said. "I just gave her the first chapter."

"Liar, liar, chicken frier," John yelled. Then he ran off and told Marybeth, who told Susie, who told Warren, who told the whole world. Soon, all the kids in the class were laughing and pointing at me. There were probably some kids laughing and pointing who *weren't* in our class.

Finally, Marybeth came over with Susie.

"This is the biggest lie Jane has ever told," said Susie.

"Is it bigger than the story about her

father being a football star?" asked Marybeth.

"Yes. It's even bigger than the one she told about her mom acting in a Broadway play," said Susie. "It's bigger because we can prove that this story is a lie."

Then she and Marybeth walked off, giggling.

Marty looked upset. "Don't listen to them, Babette," he said. "I believe you."

"It's true about the novel, Marty," I said. "But it makes no difference if you tell people the truth or not. They still don't believe you. So why should I bother?"

"Maybe it's like that fable," said Marty.

"What fable?" I said, stomping off to the edge of the playground. I didn't want to be around those creepy kids anymore.

Marty shuffled after me. He was looking at the ground. Only this time he wasn't looking for rocks.

"Remember that story about the little boy who cried wolf?" he said. Marty looked up. His face was bright red.

"You mean the one where the kid makes up so many stories about the wolf eating

81

the sheep, that when the wolf finally shows up nobody believes him?" I said.

"That's the one," said Marty. "Maybe it's like that."

"Well, I'll show them!" I said.

When we got back inside from recess, Ms. Sims was waiting for me.

"This is wonderful, Babette," she said. "Would it embarrass you to read it aloud to the class?"

"Not at all," I said. "As a matter of fact, I'd like to read the whole book to the class as I write it."

"That's a great idea," said Ms. Sims.

"I want their suggestions," I said sweetly. But that wasn't what I wanted at all.

I wanted to prove that this time, I was telling the truth. And besides, it might be fun to see how everyone felt when they figured out that *they* were the crazy, annoying kids I was writing about!

Chapter 7

*T*he next morning, Ms. Sims stood in front of the class. She waited until we were quiet. Then she said, "As some of you may know, Babette has been working on a special project. She's writing a book, and she wants to share it with you."

Warren started to laugh. Ms. Sims stared at him and he stopped.

"Why don't you come up to the front of the classroom, Babette," she said.

I stood up and walked to the front of

the class with my first chapter. I cleared my throat, took a deep breath, and started to read:

It was supposed to be a class trip like any other one—except, of course, that Mrs. Ripley's third–grade class was going to Disney World.

Mrs. Ripley was checking for lunches, sweatshirts, and permission slips when suddenly a loud voice popped up from the back of the bus.

"I don't have my lunch," said Eldridge.

"Why not?" asked Mrs. Ripley.

"I ate it on the way to school," said Eldridge.

"Why on earth did you do that?" asked Mrs. Ripley. She looked at the chubby boy over the top of her glasses.

"I was hungry," said Eldridge.

"Well, then you won't be hungry at lunchtime, will you?" said Mrs. Ripley.

"Yes, I will," said Eldridge. "I'm hungry right now!"

The kids in class started to laugh.

"That sounds just like Warren," said John Boles.

"Please don't interrupt," said Ms. Sims. But she was smiling, too. I wondered if she had figured out the truth.

I continued reading. By the time I got to the end of the chapter, everyone was all excited about the book.

Ms. Sims decided I should read the class a chapter each week from THE WORST CLASS TRIP EVER for the rest of the school year.

The kids could hardly wait to hear what was going to happen next. Some of the kids—mainly Warren Peach—actually pestered me in the playground to tell them what was going to happen next. Warren wanted to know before everyone else did.

At the end of every chapter I left the kids on the edge of a new and crazy and dangerous disaster. I had hurricanes, bad guys, wild pigs, and poisoned water holes. You name it, I stuck it in there.

I had lots of funny things happen in my book, too. Like when Karen Wiggs got lost in the jungle and we couldn't find her for two days. Marty and I tracked her down by following the sound of her sniffling!

But the funny things that happened were not just in the story, either. For one thing, I had planned to give each kid in the class a strange habit. It was going to be their weird habits that ended up saving us all, of course.

I was hoping that even though I'd changed everyone's names, they wouldn't catch on to who they were too quickly.

Well, the first surprise was that they all got it right away! Of course, with the easy ones like Marty Degan and Warren Peach, everyone figured it out in a second. Then the rest of the kids in the class guessed that they were probably in the story, too. So they started looking for themselves. By Chapter Two—when the class was driving the hijackers out of their minds—they all figured it out.

I thought the kids might be mad, but they loved it. They thought it was a great joke that their oddball acts were actually better weapons than guns and knives.

Not only that, but they started giving me ideas for the story. Marybeth sent me a zillion notes during math class.

"Why don't you have Marty go rock collecting on top of a volcano? Then I could save him before the volcano erupts."

The next note was even sillier. *"Why not have everyone get trapped in an underground water cavern? We could discover a family of mermaids!"*

During recess Marybeth came up to me. I could tell she wanted to give me some more ideas.

"If you're so good at coming up with ideas," I said to Marybeth, "why don't you write a book of your own?"

"Maybe I will!" she said. I think she was mad at me.

It turned out that she actually *did* write one over summer vacation. Nobody saw Marybeth for the whole two months.

But the very best part of all was Susie Alton.

By the time I was up to Chapter Four it was the end of May and practically the end of school. Susie came up to me on the playground.

"I want you to look at something," she said.

I was about to tell her to take a long walk off a short plank, but she looked sort of funny. For one thing, her cheeks were all red. For another, she didn't have that snooty look on her face. She was even smiling an almost regular smile.

"Sure," I said. "But I only have a minute."

She held out her sketchbook to me.

"Why are you showing me this?" I asked.

"Never mind," said Susie. She started to take it back. But I snatched it away from her. I figured she was about to show me another bunch of drawings done by a grown-up. Then she would confess that I had been right about her all along. She was just pretending to be able to draw. I could hardly wait to catch Susie Alton making up a big lie.

I opened the sketchbook. On the first page there was a picture of all the kids in our class at the gates to Disney World. There were Warren Peach, Marybeth Hughes, Ellen Winston, me, and John Boles—and, of course, Ms. Sims. The next picture showed everyone getting on the tour boat. The two guys with the long, lumpy overcoats were looking at us. Ms. Sims looked grouchy and hot.

In the next picture, all of us stood lined up against the boat cabin. The lumpy guys were holding machine guns on us. The captain and Ms. Sims had their hands up in the air. They looked really scared. Ms. Sims's glasses hung off one ear. Warren Peach was yanking on the sleeve of one of the bad guys. This was the part where Warren kept saying, "When is lunch?"

These pictures were great!

"You did these?" I asked as I flipped through a few more. But I knew the answer.

"Uh-huh," said Susie, looking sort of snooty, but still red-faced.

The rest of the pictures matched the story, right up through Chapter Four.

"When did you draw them?" I asked.

"I did some of them while you were reading out loud to us," Susie said. "But most of them I drew at home, from what I remembered."

"I bet," I said. I tried to sound like I didn't think they were so great.

Actually, I was really pleased. But I didn't want to tell Susie that. After all, I'd accused her of lying about being able to draw. These pictures looked like a grown-up's work, but Susie was the only person who could have done them.

The only grown-ups who had heard the story were Ms. Sims and my mom. Neither of them could draw at all. Susie had just proved she was telling the truth.

Of course, I had been proving for the last month that I was telling the truth about writing a real novel.

So there we were. I wasn't a liar anymore. And Susie wasn't a liar either. We were artists! How neat!

"Let's go inside and show your drawings to Ms. Sims," I said, still holding on to the sketchbook.

Susie tried to grab the book back. "No! They're not good enough to show her yet."

"Sure they are," I said. "I think Ms. Sims will really like them."

We walked back inside together. Ms. Sims was sitting at her desk correcting papers. She glanced up from her desk when we entered the room. "Ms. Sims," I said, "we have something to show you."

Susie walked slowly to the front of the classroom and handed her the sketchbook. Her face was bright red.

Ms. Sims spent a long time studying the pictures. Then she looked up at Susie. "Your drawings are excellent, Susie."

Susie smiled. And I did, too. I was really glad Ms. Sims liked the pictures.

Ms. Sims thought for a minute. Then she said, "I have an idea. Why don't you put the drawings and the story together? Then we can make photocopies. That way, all of the class can have their own copy of the story to remember our third-grade year."

"That's great!" I cried. "All I have to do now is finish it!"

And I did—or I should say, *we* did. We finished it just before the last day of school.

With Susie drawing pictures right along

with me, I got really excited. I began thinking about what each part of the story should *look* like. I wanted to write good scenes for Susie to draw.

Of course, that meant Susie and I had to talk to each other a lot.

And guess what?

Susie and I are best friends now.

It turns out that she's just like me. I mean, her mom and dad are divorced, too. But it's worse for her. Her dad got married again and actually started a whole new family! At least my mom and dad have the sense to keep it simple.

And Susie was snooty to me because she thought *I* was stuck up. I guess I *was* acting stuck up, too.

Having a best friend was great. We worked, and we talked, and we played together all the time. And I didn't have to make up even one story! The truth could actually be pretty interesting, too.

By the time the last day of school came in June, the book was done and so were all the pictures.

I got everyone off the island. I got the

bad guys arrested. We had already started driving the Coast Guard crazy on the boat that rescued us in the last chapter.

In the book, Ms. Sims was very grateful to all of us. She promised that since we had saved her life—I had her step on a piece of coral and get poisoned—she would never give us any homework again.

We said she could give us all the homework she wanted, but that she wasn't allowed to give anyone a lower grade than a B + .

All we wanted, we said, was another chance to take a trip to Disney World!

So here we are, Susie and I and the rest of the class, headed for fourth grade. We'll be rich and famous by then, I'm sure. You see, I sent a copy of the book to this famous Hollywood director. Maybe he'll want to make it into a movie. And he'll want everyone in the class to be in it. I can just see Susie and me riding to school next year in a limousine.

I feel sort of sorry for our fourth-grade teacher.

Wouldn't you?